ME AND MY FATHER'S JOURNEY

BY: NWANKWO MISHAD

Art of the Author Publishing
P.O. Box 521
Hampton, GA 30228

HARSH REALITIES

I was born a spoiled child, but not spoiled with gifts, material, or money. I was spoiled with love. See my father loved me like no other, so he showed it to me through his actions. He never bragged nor wanted praise, but just wanted to do his job.

At the same time, he was a jealous man. He was jealous of my father and the relationship we had, and the bond we shared. My father didn't like our bond, because his father wasn't like mine. Therefore, every time he saw my father close to me, he would have this look in his eyes as if he wished he had this type of attention when he was my age.

One day when my father was alone with me, he stopped me to say," Son, I'm battling this other man, the man that was abandoned by his father, the man that wished he had this same kind of love from his father". Therefore, he hugged me tight and kissed me on the forehead then said, "Son, I love you and reality is that I'm jealous of our relationship. I am the man I wanted my father to be. So, I spoil you with my attention that the other half of me never received".

THE TABLE OF CONTENTS

PREFACE

The idea of this book, *Me and My Father's Journey,* has been on my mind for (two) years. A major part of this book comes from the emptiness I've had within myself, and what I've seen with different individuals throughout my life. In this book, I want to influence those that have been lost as a child, but most importantly, those lost adults that are seeking the guidance based on a troubled childhood. My childhood was different than most, but mentally I've overcame many distractions that would influence my future.

This book is fiction, but the story line is genuine based on everyday life. I began the book with a poem personally written by myself, because of a lost father that was confused on how to deal with a situation within himself. I title the poem, *Harsh Realities;* initially this poem was written within 15 seconds based on a conversation with a special friend on the phone. Harsh Realities are what we are faced with every day, but confused minds of father's is why most children grow up without one. The father in the poem has a backwards way of thinking, because his emotions confused his mind. This was a poem I thought was important, because most men especially so-called

African Americans deal with this struggle day to day. Our parent's teachings whether they're in our lives or not have influenced how most of us think as parents.

In writing this book, I want to talk directly and personally to you, my readers, to include: fathers, mothers, children, and non-parents. I want this book to touch all races, ages, religions, and economic backgrounds. As you read the story of the lessons the main character talks about, or ways to make life and parenting fun with being patient throughout life; I encourage you to take heed that everything in life will be a lesson learned, whether it is a good or bad situation. Many children around the world need a positive influence and are seeking that attention from somewhere if not home. Make your situation a learning situation and inspire your children that you can give them a better life than what you've had, and how to overcome obstacles. I hope this book influence you in some way and touch many lives as possible.

A NIGHT TO REMEMBER
Chapter 1

"Prince" was a name that my father has given me since birth, because he cherished the thought of having a son. As an infant, I automatically knew who my father was by his scent; Winter-fresh breath with a strong, but sweet mist from his body cologne. A deep vibration from his mouth welcomed me in with, "Hello my Prince", as he looked down to me surprised with having his first born. He embraced me with love as he cut this long string from my belly button. I was 6 pounds and 11 ounces with sparkling brown hair; also, I noticed the glare from his white teeth that he was excited to see me. His hands were rough, but gentle as he held my hands with one finger. As I screamed my lungs out, he soothed me with songs that he knew would calm me down. He hummed in harmony as if he could really sing.

My mom was asleep most of that night, so it felt like my father and I danced the night away. The hospital room was full of colors that glared from the light shining off balloons and window curtains. The noise of a train riding throughout the night calmly sent me to sleep in my father's arms. Waking up in the middle of the night crying from hunger, I realized my father never put me down even when he had the chance. That night at the hospital was a night to remember, because I knew my father was going to protect me for the rest of my life. Warmth and comfort was what I felt, as his eyes told it all with no blink but seriousness as if he knew what presence he would lead.

The next morning my mom woke-up with a big smile on her face knowing that she would have that support she needed, because the way she looked at my father displayed confidence within her heart. A father and son bond couldn't be broken, like a strong mind that's tampered with in an injustice world. Happily as a family, our chemistry was molded into one. Breakfast was served and the nurses and doctors evaluated my mom and me for one last time before we were sent home. The smell of fresh flowers and weird chirping noises struck my attention as we were leaving out the exit doors waiting on my father to drive around to us. My mother said to me "Son we will always have a bond, and I will always love you". I guess her ways of telling me goodbye. . After that day, in a house that I thought was full of comfort and love; Arguments and fights disturbed me from getting my rest.

Most parents have fear in them when their children are brought into the world, but it takes a real parent to overcome that obstacle. I had no idea on how to be a child and he didn't know how to be a parent, so I guess we had to teach each other as we were going through the process. Children learn everything from their parents, which teaches parents how to overcome distractions with multi-tasking. Patience is everything, because we're brought into the world as the most selfish individuals.

My father has been a big influence in my life that will be indebted in me for the rest of my life. Life situations caused me to have a rocky childhood that I really haven't understood until I've gotten older. I grew up in a single parent household, but unlike most children, my father raised me. I remember my father dragging me along everywhere trying to reach deadlines of employment offerings, turning down jobs that couldn't function around our schedule, paying bills that we barely had the money for, or watching my father cry because of situations he was forced to be in whether good or bad.

Understanding my father then was an overstatement that couldn't be accomplished. However, our struggles forced us to be inseparable. We made the best of everything, and every dime my father had was given to me. Of course, I was stubborn, disobedient, and cried when my selfish ways were over looked. Every child has those days when we irritate our parents just because we can, but our parents have an unconditional love that helps them tolerate us.

My father grew up worse than I did, and his father was in and out of his life like a DVD that skipped and played when it felt. As great as a father he was to me, abandonment was something I would have never thought he faced. He rather wore a chip on his shoulders, because he was determine not to fail me most importantly himself. Most men/women make excuses for their circumstances and want people to feel sorry for them with a handout. He was not a perfect man, but he was what I looked up too so he was perfect to me. He embodied so much negativity in his life, that he didn't want me to inherent the same life or mistakes. My mom was that DVD in my life she made every excuse she could think of ever since my birth.

I haven't held her accountable for my circumstances, but expected more out of her since she carried me for nine months. She grew up with both parents and a loving household, but turned out to be the total opposite of what she saw her parents do. My father tried so hard not to allow me to follow in his shoes, but it somewhat backfired with my mother not having the same mindset as him. It allowed him to be stuck in his tracks, because he wanted a family that he never had. Love was a feeling that I've had for both of my parents; being that it was unconditional; I loved and hated them at the same time.

Remembering my mother goodbyes allowed me to question my presence for being on earth. I haven't understood my family since, because they were just pretending to be happy thinking I was going to keep us all together. I felt like I was the reason for all the mayhem, because of the destruction after I was born. It was nothing like family was what I thought, as I saw how we coincided with each other. I learned from that point that nothing could keep a family together, not even a child.

Despite my circumstances with my mom, her voice was always remembered. Random phone calls always made me warm inside, with a chill that made me nervous every time I heard her voice. She ended every phone call with a kiss and said "I love you baby". It always given me mixed feelings, as I have gotten older, because what kind of woman would abandon her own child, and what was her real reason for leaving.

The destruction divided my family into two separate households. People force themselves to be in relationships and began to live the rest of their lives miserable, but if that happiness isn't there, just make a way to make is better or leave it alone. Some relationships are better apart, because they hinder you from what your life is actually suppose to be. We will always love each other I see, but separation could make a family stronger or the jealousy of one could sour the initial reason of calling it a family.

FIRST TIME JITTERS
Chapter 2

My father having to start from scratch put us in a rebuilding stage. Our relationship was rocky, because we were feeding off each other's energy. My stubborn ways didn't help our situation, because I always wanted things my way and refused to compromise. We were like best friends, because we fussed, played, learned, and laughed with each other all the time.

It's frustrating being a parent on your own, but my ways were not being answered when I wanted them to so I acted out to seek the attention I needed. "Son could you please help me out" is what my father said frequently throughout our relationship, because I disobeyed orders knowing it would agitate him. We know more than our parents realize, but we are stuck in our ways a lot. I laughed when I saw my father sweat extra from running around chasing me to put on my diaper and urine shot out into the air when he took too long changing me. We both laughed, because he knew that I was smarter than the average child was. He never baby talked me, but talked to me as if we were both human beings which helped me comprehend faster.

Going to different department stores, restaurants, or parks people would stop us just to baby talk me as if I knew what they were saying, so I screamed as loud as possible so they could get away from me. People should always wonder why babies look at them crazy while their talking silly with the different languages as if we understand baby talk. When you talk normal to babies the smarter they become, because it develops children to talk in complete sentences. One thing about my father is that he always has given me the respect that I've deserved no matter how much I fussed with him. The look on my father's face sometimes was priceless, because he stayed calm through all my troubles I brought to him. He potty trained me alone with the exception of the help of daycare, but I gave him the worst time of his life knowing that he was trying.

My father soon enrolled me into daycare, which gave me the opportunity to be around others like me. The smell of fresh diapers, baby wipes, and baby lotion was always a home feeling. I attached myself to every woman that came along my way, because they were more of a motherly figure that I missed. That sweet and warmth feeling that makes me dissolve into a baby when they nurtured me with love. My father did the best he could, but it was nothing like the feeling of a mother. It was a cold and empty feeling, as if my mom left me at an abandoned building, and I waited on her while screaming her name and no one there to answer me. I wasn't fully potty trained at that moment, but how sweet these women were made me give in and listen to them as they told me when to use the bathroom. My father never complained being that he was a little hard on me, which made me be harder on him. I was now fully potty trained and used what I was taught to become more independent.

Women at the daycare admired my father, because men like him didn't exist. A single father these days were uncommon. A single father was like saying Christopher Columbus discovered America, it was a heard of opportunity that couldn't be proven. Of course, he was a single father, but people treated him differently. Red carpets were at our convenience, because people just wanted to help. At the same time, people didn't think a man could raise a child, so they would give him a hard time. A handout was something that people wanted when they didn't want to try in life, and still try to live above their means. My father worked hard to establish a better life for us, which is why he needed the help but didn't beg to receive it and also was too proud to accept gifts.

A jitter was something everybody received which is butterflies, especially not knowing the outcome of how things in life were going to evolve. Of course, the thought of being a parent gives you butterflies as if you were in front of a crowd giving a speech. A single parent is a big step, especially coming from a father that never had a leader to follow. Society allowed men to stay in a box, and sealed our ways of thinking.

Most men refuse try to step up, because of the fear that started during slavery days. The mentality is still there, but some men try to break out of the stereotype. I haven't realized it then, but I didn't know how to be a son either. As much as my father was going through obstacles trying to please me, I felt the same way in return. How do I become a good child?, What if I wasn't who my father wanted as a son/child?, or What if I fail as a child?; Were some of the questions I had in my mind. Being the first at anything make you evaluate your reason of doing things, which scares most of us into not completing the task.

Ring! Ring! Ring! The alarm sounded, as my father entered my room. "Rise and shine son and welcome to the real world", I never understood those words until now. I was entering a new chapter of my which was the first day of head start as it came fast, but I was willing to take on this new challenge. "Use the bathroom, Brush your teeth, take a shower, put on your clothes," my father ordered. Early morning preparation was something I would I've gotten use to eventually, because my father was strict making should things were done correct. I begged my father months before to let me ride the school bus. I saw the children looked happy as if they were excited about going to school. It's a saying "be careful what you ask for" that stuck in my head from that point forward.

As I headed down the stairs from freshening up and preparing for school, I noticed my father reading a newspaper entitled "Final Call" which struck my attention from that morning and throughout my childhood. My father always read, but I never knew what he did as a career. I knew he was a businessman that wore bow ties and suits, but never knew his business. We ate breakfast and headed off to school. My school wasn't far so my dad walked me every morning. Walking was our way to converse amongst each other with a peaceful mind, and keep each other up-to-date about what's new in our lives.

On our way to school, I noticed my father glancing down at me through the lens of his glasses. "What daddy?" I asked. "I'm proud of you, because you are such a mature young man at the age of three", he replied. My father had been so hard on me to prepare me for this moment. The glaze in his eye has reminded me of the moment he first held me. He knew that I paid attention to him since the day I was born, and we needed each other no bigger than the next. An equal bond we shared was irreplaceable, and no one can take it away. The importance of our miscommunication and my disobedience were to keep us closer together with him being patient enough to teach me right from wrong. Being brought into the world with different characters of human beings may cause confusion. We are never alike and that's what makes up the equality, because opposites connect if you are willing to do so.

CHORES OF ACTIVITIES
Chapter 3

"Progression is a transition that takes time to accomplish."

-Nwankwo Mishad

My father was molding me into a man by gradually with taking baby steps. The more he tried to teach me the less I recognized his motives, because of my stubborn ways. Responsibility was a step that most children failed to accomplish, because we rely on our parents or other individuals to accomplish things for us.

I was taught the ideal of responsibility of a man, when my father owned up to be my primary parent. It's a lot of character of determination when you take on a big task of any sort. As I've gotten older grooming and organization was important to my father. Organizing your life is a chore that must be kept up-to-date. A man/woman that cannot take care of himself or herself is a "lazy mind" my father would say continuously.

Police sirens were a common music that played through my city. It was so normal I barely realized the loud noise, because I was immune to it. Most individuals tend to rely on their environments to dictate their futures, so that is why most try to obtain an image just to fit in with people around them. My father was strict, but it was needed in my environment due to the reality we were exposed too.

Realizing the type of environment we were in, made me think a lot about how my future was going to evolve. Every morning I woke up with a routine that I followed: make up my bed, straighten my room, iron my clothes, and freshen up. Most household lack rules, and that's one reason why police sirens is a common music in cities like mine. My neighborhood had an unusual scent of smoke in the air from gunpowder, and gave a visual of half-dressed women being promiscuous to the young businessmen standing on the corner hustling for their lives. Day after day, I saw the same routines with no sense of leadership, substance, or guidance.

The next morning sun shined extra bright, birds chirping and the noise of grass cut woke me up from a wonderful nights rest. A deep voice from the outside of my window startled me, "Wake up we have some work to do", my father said. I wasn't warned ahead of time of what was going to take place the following day. My clothes set aside my bed gave me an idea of the activity that was going to occur. Gardening, it was something different, because most men now a day lost sight on what kept so-called African Americans grounded to ownership. Surprises were always wonderful, because it made our days fun.

Receiving one-on-one leadership or mentorship from a man I admired and looked up to was remarkable. Clean overalls turned into brown and oily rags with grass stains that blended through our blue jean fabric. Cold lemonade set our energy to a higher level from the sun piercing through our skin. We spent so much time talking, laughing, and learning that we never noticed how fast time went by.

Our neighbors didn't understand what was taking place in our household, because laughter was their ignorant ways of expressing themselves. They looked as if they never saw a father and son united. Stupidity was what some considered smart, because they judge you from your looks and not what your personality have to offer. Gunshots and dead bodies were their ways of expressing themselves. My father mentored some of the children in the neighborhood, but the neighborhood lacked the support that my father was trying to establish. An active father wasn't a normal in my neighborhood, which made me resist him. I rebelled against him sometimes to prevent him from being affectionate around my friends. It changed my way of thinking a little, because children teased me on how strict and loving my father was and they put our relationship in a category as abnormal.

Cutting grass, planting flowers, pulling weeds, and grooming the outer layers of where the grass begins wasn't a woman's job. A true family make sure home is taken care of, because this is where you lay your head every night. Of course, demandingly my father had his ways of bargaining, but overall we got the job done. He was more excited to teach, than I was willing to learn. Once the yard was finished, we cleaned up, and had a chance to relax as we saw our accomplished work.

Preparing a meal later that night was easy after seeing my father do it consecutively throughout the years. We first set the table as if we had multiple guests coming for dinner. "Forks, spoons, and knives are kept in a certain way always remember that" my father said as held my hand and proceeded to grab the plates. Making chores an activity of fun will prepare you better than making it a serious matter. Most children think responsibility is a form of punishment depending on how the parent instructs it, so it taught me organization before and after I eat.

The aroma of fresh stemmed broccoli, baked salmon topped with fresh mozzarella with onions and bell peppers, bean soup, and a fresh bean pie for dessert from the brothers in black suits and bow ties standing on the corners made me anxious to eat before we cooked. "Always cook for yourself, so you won't have to depend on another individual," my father said. "Was life really this difficult or what was my father preparing me for?" I asked myself. Having fun cooking could always make a household interesting. After dinner, we brushed our teeth and settled for bed. "Son do you know why I teach you small things" he asked, "No dad" I replied. "So when you get older they won't be big things," he stated. It made sense in many ways, because looking at my friends households made me appreciate what I had a home. Organization might not be a bad thing, we just lack at doing it, which make us pay for consequences in the future. Living life with a purpose is what I was learning, but I was tested to see how my father's methods were going transpire in my life.

Responsibility keeps us out of trouble, because we desperately look for a sense of guidance to lead us to the right path. African Americans are the most divided race, because organization and responsibility was derived from our households. One resolution to dissolve our problems in our neighborhoods is to make a difference and not materialize ourselves, but look for a better purpose. My father isn't perfect, but tried his best to teach me the importance of life. Listening to my father will be the success, and failure will be taking a different path than what I'm taught. We all have choices, so which road are we considering to take and that could lead to good consequences or bad consequences that results from our decisions.

THE TEACHING
CHAPTER 4

41 | P a g e

I was blessed to have a father around, but most households scrabbled to find a male figure and that normally symbolizes their broken mood-swings. He has taught me so much in my past years that allowed me to be who I am today. I'm now headed into my middle school years, in which starts at the sixth grade level. Peer pressure, harder work, puberty, and most important more children, which symbolized personalities from all lifestyles in one building.

Cycles repeated overtime, because this was similar to my preschool days. Nervous gut feelings demoralized the way I felt about waking up each day. Urgency was going to play big role in how I was going to further my education. In my head, all I could hear is a voice from my father, "Take heed to why you are here"; it rang through my ears, like an alarm when the snooze button is repeatedly pressed. The order of how to demand a person respect is through their presentation. How you present yourself tells a lot about that individual, so my confidence and presence outweighed my butterflies.

Two weeks before my first day of school, my father wanted to do a different type of shopping with me. "Wake up son we have some business to take care of", he said. I had to take a long stretch and yawn, and proceeded to roll out of my bed. Immediately, I freshened up and did my normal morning routine. After putting on my clothes, I advanced downstairs and headed to the car. As I stepped up to get into the vehicle, I began to buckle my seat belt, but notice giggling coming from my father. "Dad what's funny" I asked. "Just seeing you grow up so fast is unreal," he replied. I guess when being around your children everyday distracts a parent from seeing the actual growth process, because they're too busy molding them into young adults. Sometimes I wished my mother were here to see me grow into a man. My mother wasn't dead, but it felt like it by her not giving me a sign that she was here with me.

We pulled up to the department store, after a ride that seemed like we drove forever. A man well dressed greeted us at our car as we waited in line. "Good Evening Gentleman", said the man as he spoke with an accent. Having a valet to greet us at a clothing store was unheard of, but it made me feel like a king. We stepped out of our vehicle and headed into the fancy department store. Suits, button down shirts, pleaded slacks, Dobb hats, pointed and square tip shoes, and bow ties were the making of man. A well-dressed man has more confidence, and it brings him attention of respect from everyone that glances his way. Walking into the store made me feel different as if I was somebody. The person will make the clothes, but sometimes the clothes can inspire you into another element.

The experience of trying on all these clothes made me evaluate our living arrangements. My father took me to an expensive store, but we stay in a rural environment. We were treated as if we have been here before. Meanwhile, I was still nervous about my first day of school, but this day eased my mind. We prepared to leave the store after trying on clothes and getting measured for pants and shirt sizes. It was a comfortable feeling trying on these clothes and it made me feel better about myself.

We arrived home and something in my mind inspired me to read. I had a completely new attitude about myself. Walking into the house I tempted to go to my father's bookshelf and grab whatever book I could find. I grabbed a thick heavy biography entitled "Denmark Vesey" that stood out the most, so sat down at the table and proceeded to read. "Daddy I want to read this book, but can't figure out what it's talking about". "Son its okay everyone have a problem comprehending words, so I will help you", my father said as he pulled his glasses down and laughed. A sense of humor is what my father lived with, because little things never bothered him. A person can't stress over what they can't control. As I got clarification on who Denmark Vesey was, I gained more confidence, because of what he stood for. The fearless attitude inspired me, because he was a king in my eyes as well as me.

My first day of class was underway, and I was prepared for my new beginning. Waking up this particular morning was different, because I was confused on how my school year was going to begin. New shoes, clothes, hairstyles, and fresh school supply is what invited people to go to school. My new mindset has inspired me to make sure I learned something new on my first day and days to come. Oral Communications was a class I wasn't looking forward to, because talking in front of people made me uncomfortable. In my mind, I was discouraged, because this was an important class. My teacher was an older woman with strong perfume, red lip stick, Gray curly hair, and a smile that made you want to only say nice things about her.

Before class ended we had to introduce ourselves, and our teacher had thrown us a homework assignment just because she loved her job. "A SPEECH!" is what I yelled in my head as she announced our homework assignment that was based on our views of life. I was not prepared to have any homework assignments on my first day, but to make it worse a speech.

After my long day of school, I enter the house excited to be home. My father was sitting on the couch reading his "Final Call" newspaper. He pulled the top of the paper down, because he wanted to take a full look at me. "Son how was school and what's with the long face", he asked. I told him about the speech, and how I felt about my teacher. He stopped me as I furthered the conversation. "This is the real world and you have to apply yourself and if not you will be just a statistic", he responded. Being prepared for everything will allow me to calm down, and allowed life to show me things. This class was more of a life teaching, because it helped gain my courage and confidence, which prepare me for life. A wise father I had, but if I did not apply, what he was teaching me, then it would be pointless for him to help.

Restless nights allowed me to think, because I was overwhelmed with a speech that kept me up until the next morning. My mind was racing; the thought of freezing up and what if my voice showed I was nervous or afraid. Made me have second-guesses about if I should play sick that day of school. The sunset and I was still tossing and turning. My father wakes up early every morning, and always checks on me before he walk down the stairs and read his paper. As he walked passed my room and noticed I was moving, "You up sleepy head", he asked. "Yes couldn't sleep, but I'm up", I replied.

After rolling out of bed, I put on some shorts and proceeded down stairs. I stepped onto the porch, because it looked very windy outside on this sunny day. My father followed behind me with a note from relatives about a family meeting. We had been away from family for a while which made me anxious to see them and what new stories we were going to hear. My dad always gave a speech, because they always listened to him with his role on our family committee. He prepared a speech that he spent writing the night before, which was the length of one page or two. He asked me to hear him read it, and asked me to read it back to him so he can see how it sounds.

The next morning, we packed up our clothes and got in the car, and proceeded to drive to our family meeting. On our way there, I was taught how to paraphrase, so I will not have to read word by word. Thinking of speaking in another element like paraphrasing never crossed my mind, but it made perfect sense. Meanwhile, we arrived at the building where our meeting. A tall brick building with a nice lawn and flowers surrounded it. An emblem that held stars and a crescent moon stood out, because it felt like we were in the presence of gods as we entered. Other family members as they stood excited waiting for everyone to arrive greeted us at the door. One of my favorite Aunts kissed me on the cheek with joy, and grabbed my hand as we walked around to greet everyone. The feel of love was in the room and most of it came my way. Everyone finally arrived, so the program was beginning to start. The purpose of the meeting was to allow our family businesses to develop more money.

My father stood up and proceeded towards the podium, because he was the lead speaker of our meeting. He started by greeting everyone, and then asked me to join him. In my mind I thought, "Why do I have to come up here, or what does he want now?" I walked up and stood next to my father as he talked, and he asked me to read the speech we prepared. My heart dropped, because how could he catch me off guard with no preparation within myself. I took a deep breath with no hesitation and began with the speech. The fear I thought I had was gone, and it felt good to be comfortable speaking. When you prepare yourself for anything-in life, it allows you to stay ready. It taught me that I could do anything that I am afraid of doing.

My father taught me how to be prepared no matter the circumstances, because you never know when your time will come. The energy in the room was very positive and made me want to do it again. My lesson was to know what you talking about, because you have to persuade people into how you feel while speaking. There was no coincidence on why I had to speak, because it prepared me for life and my homework assignment. Courage is something that is in you, but it takes a special person to help bring it out.

My speech for school was easy after my encounter at my family event, because I knew my family prepared me for the better. After my speech for school, my classmates gave me a standing ovation due to how organized my speech was, and my stage presence. Our teacher was very pleased, so I knew my school year was going to be on the right track.

Your presentation is what will get people attention, and then how you carry yourself is the icing on the cake. Learning how to dress, and look good doing it is just part of having confidence. Your attitude and how you talk makes a human being complete. You will always have butterflies when you step to a challenge, because we are human. How you take on that challenge will determine who you are and where you will end up in life.

TESTING THE RECREATION
Chapter 5

Being black in the world I live in is sometimes hard, especially an intelligent black male that thinks and read. Some of us are fortunate to be athletic and dominate in sports that we participate in. We live in a habitat that causes us to be immune to one main success, which are sports. Liquor stores, pretty women, gun shops, street hustlers, users, dealers, and petty thugs were reasons that made us play sports just to stay out of trouble. Genetically, we are athletic by nature, but in our world, we are over weighed by sports than our natural talent, which is education.

As I've reached new age brackets, respect and honor is what my father gained from me. I haven't realized the presence my father stood for, until I saw how fathers of some of my classmates were absent from their lives. Reaching an age where I understood sports due to watching my father chant, and also yell when games were reversed from how he thought they would go. Driving around town seeing basketball courts filled with 5 on 5 or 3 on 3 pick-up games made me interested.

In my neighborhood, football games like: Jackpot, rumble fumble, and two hand touches were what we looked forward to in order to buy time. Getting chased by dogs and playing "NicKnock" on neighbors doors were our ways of getting ready for track. Street fights that made a man out of those that were brutally beaten, or diminished their souls to be weak prepared us for boxing. We had ways of making fun out of everything, but time was winding down with how much I wanted to be like my father.

My father was an All-American in every sport that he participated in, which inspired me to be better than him. "Dad" I yelled from the other room. "Yes Prince", he replied taking off his apron as he was preparing dinner. "I think I want to learn how to play sports", I said. "Ok when you want to start and what sport?" my father replied with a smile. "All of them" I responded. He always supported my decisions, but this was more of a proud father moment. He always wanted me to play sports, due to the distractions I was faced with every day. "First thing in the morning we will start son" he stated.

I admired his athletic background; he once scored 6 touchdowns with 356 yards rushing, and his football team scored Eighty-eight points on one team that mark them in the history books for his state. His track, baseball, basketball, and soccer ability was unquestioned. A big shoe to follow was my thought, but I was willing to take the challenge. Being the first player in his school history to have twenty-three full-ride scholarships in different sports, with twenty-six academic scholarship offered was very impressive.

Everything I wanted to be and more, but I knew it wasn't going to just come to me easily. He would always tell me to make sure my grades were excellent, because with knowledge people can't deny you from what you earned. Most athletes were owned and had to demote themselves to something they wasn't, so it taught me to treat everything like a business because I knew my worth. His rookie card still sits on my nightstand from when he went pro in football.

The next morning, I woke up super excited and anxious about what I was going to learn. It was a misty morning, but it was perfect in the summer season. My father was still sleeping, which gave me the honor to wake him up. He knew I was serious, especially noticing that I was already dressed. Thirty minutes later we were set and ready to head outside. As we arrived on the lawn we sat down to have a talk. "It's more than life than sports son. Knowledge comes first and I don't want you to forget that", he said.

I always dreamed about being on television with everyone chanting my name. Walking before crawling was what I wanted to do, but I knew rushing anything in life wasn't going to end well. A wise man is what I stood next to, because he always challenged my way of thinking. Every child needs this kind of push in order to be humble. Getting things handed to us will always have a price behind it. Meanwhile, we stood up and took a walk through our neighborhood. His idea of teaching me about sports was not what I expected. "We are going to have a reality check before we continue our session" he said.

As we walked through the neighborhood I noticed how bad our environment really was. A lot of athletes flooded our community, but are now hook on needles and bottles. A community with such high hopes for certain individuals, but yet and still they couldn't prove that they were serious about what they really wanted. Former athletes also turned to dealing drugs to their friends, and bragging about the benefits they materialized on. Our world and our communities were so much in bad shape was what I thought, because I knew my community wasn't the only one. The outlook my father showed me help me realize how big my dream was. We continue our session with roaming through the neighborhood, but finished with baseball, boxing, basketball, football, and how to run track.

Fundamentals and technique was the importance of us going outside in which we need them in everyday life. It was meant for me to ask my father to teach me, because he showed me how important my dream really was. We never know who we are talking to when we see addicts or alcoholics. We see their circumstances and think they are who they are, but technically they were you at one point. Their dream wasn't capitalized due to their minds and decisions they've made. Given a new outlook on sports allowed me to work harder at everything that was put forth to me. The reason my father stressed "knowledge and education", because it's what we will need when we finish our role in sports. Paying attention to your environment and also the sports world will educate you for what it really means. Sports aren't granted to everyone, so find out who we are and know that fundamentals and technique carries us through the decisions we make throughout life.

SIB-LITTLE (Little Sibling)
Chapter 6

We took road trips consisting of bright lights and mellow music, which lead to pitch black grassy fields with animals howling to the glare of the moon light. Addicted to our glorified precious moments that couldn't be replaced was what made me selfish, and provided a protection for my father's love. My father gave me countless talks, and we gave each other our undivided attention as we taught each other how to live life. Memory lane on our special moments together: Potty training, first steps, first days of school, etc... That led us to this point. I loved a father that sacrificed so much for me, which was hard to share. My appreciation towards him was for what he stood for, but it felt like it was gone in the midst of a second. The feeling was like I lost both of my parents within years even though my father was here physically.

My father had been dating a woman for years now, and decided to take it more serious. Every time I saw them around each other his smile was bigger each time, because he was happy and showed his love for her every chance he got. My input was invalid, so the woman stole my heart and of course my father's. I never saw my father this happy, which gave me the confusion on how I felt. Long walks we took together with a chemistry that we been missing influenced me to lack my decision of mistreating her. She treated me like I was her child and spoiled me with love and gifts. When she tried talking to me I treated her with a cold shoulder, because she wasn't my mother and I didn't want to hear what she had to say. "Why doesn't he like me" is what I walked in on as she was talking to my father. My guilt sunk through my body, because this nice woman granted me something that I never had and I disliked her for no reason. Why my mother just couldn't be here and make it easier for me. It was like I was still holding on to a position that will never get filled.

The absent love of my mother sinks so deep through my skin that my knees were weak and my body quenched for love from emptiness. Accepting love from another woman had a pain that ate through me, because I was selfish not wanting someone to take my mother's secret place. Having another woman in my presence made me deceptive of my father. How could he bring a woman into my life and not allow me to approve, nor allow my mother to be granted a decision. The resistance from me forced a bitter home with tension that was confused. I disliked the woman I starred at basically, because she wasn't the woman I wanted in my life. Allowing one woman an open key to my heart was priceless, but my mother never accepted that key and left it on a doorstep for another soul to steal. A thief through the night is how I looked at it, but she was everything she was everything I wanted my mother to be.

One morning my father entered the house with a surprise that will change my life. "Son take a seat we need to talk", he said with a curious face. The starred look I gave my father was clueless, because this meeting involved his girlfriend. Bittersweet taste in my mouth because these were moments we shared, but she included herself as if we were a family. "We are having a baby" they said together.

I had a speechless moment thinking that not only I have to share my father with a woman, but now it's a silly baby. The thought of another selfish human being made me sick to my stomach.

Jealousy soaked in, but I thought about a more positive aspect. Having someone I could boss around would be nice, or would it be mean. I could use this opportunity to mentor, so that we could grow close. Many more thoughts entered my head and kept me puzzled, because I didn't know how to talk to my father at this point. Our small circle we shared just expanded, but I had found a way to keep my family together. "Dad can I talk to you", I pleaded. "Of course son, What's Up", he responded.

We begin to talk about how our family was going to change and then he said, "Son, I'm going to need you more than ever. Our relationship will never change and I agree with how you're perceiving things, but you will be the importance in our family that we have established". Importance was the keyword that I heard in that sentence, which made me feel important to take on a responsibility.

As the months continued, my baby sister was ready to visit the world. Her moments were different than mine, because she actually had a mother that was happy to see her. Jealousy sparked again, because I wanted this all along. The blessing of my sister entering this earth was priceless, but hearing her cry made me lose all negative thoughts and appreciate my step-mom. Realizing how much a woman put up with just by having a baby humbled me to how much respect I had for this woman. "Do you want to hold her Prince?" my step-mom asked. "Yes I will hold my baby sister Justice" I responded.

Getting the privilege to name her was an honor, because I finally received justice for my life. My perception was neither woman nor man can determine an outcome of your life. Sometimes you have to take what's given to you and roll with it. We never asked to come to this world, nor who do we want our parents to be. People are brought into this world for good and bad reasons, especially not knowing their initial intentions.

My step-mom was brought to my father to show me that love is really here on earth, and my sister showed me that anything can inspire a change. Taking heed to my surrounding I know how much of an impact that I would become. A new beginning with new goals that I want to set forth. A mother's love couldn't be replaced, but it could be substituted with someone with better intensions. My mother will never be forgotten, but sometimes in my life I will have to make choices for my happiness. No longer will my pass determine my future, and for once and for all justice is serve to those who need redemption for a soul that's incomplete.

EYE'S LIKE MINE
Chapter 7

Realizing the impact I've had on another human being with my presence allowed me to continue to be positive. Establishing a new foundation to build off of brings a feeling of hope, because seeing my sister smile was priceless. Analyzing my life brought me to think that I have someone that looks up to me, and soon will mimic every step that I take. My sister and I really haven't had a full conversation, but our chemistry told it all. Refusing to allow my sister to feel how I felt growing up was my main goal. Making a difference to someone may help my life also despite of my pain. We never know how often the little things we do that changes a person perspective on how they view things, no matter what that individual may have been through. I'm glad that I have the opportunity to start inspiring at the beginning of someone life.

Growing up in a lower class neighborhood brought me closer to my little sister, due to the violence that took place around us. The thought of being a protector when my father wasn't around was my duty. The leader that taught me everything stood over to make sure I was doing things properly. Besides my father attending his duties as a parent, I wanted to also let my presence be known. No real obligation, but I just wanted to return the favor to someone I know will need my guidance in the future. Trust was what I had to gain, because as selfish as we are as children loyalty is what we confined to. If my father wasn't loyal I wouldn't have as much respect as I do for him, so I had to be consistent to her.

Being a big brother was a challenging role, because it is very important. My sister's keeper is what I had to be. Knowing that our parent's will not be around all our lives, forced me to start as soon as possible. Leading by example allows a person to see your words coming to life. In order to lead you have to follow, so following behind my father prepared me for what's yet to come. Days after school and football practice consisted of brotherly duties which were: play, diaper changing, feeding, and more playing. Her potty training days were up, so she walked around with more confidence. Our days were planned for us as if we knew how to communicate through spirit.

Sand boxes filled with toys and sand castles on sunny peaceful days, allowed us to imagine that it was just the two of us in the place we called life. Reality set in when neighborhood children would ruin our moments trying to take over our play dates. Protecting us was an order that had to be granted in the neighborhood we were surrounded in. Fighting was no tolerance with my father, but he understood that boys would be boys. My father treated me with the love and respect that other's wasn't privileged to have, so it forced us to blend in with different backgrounds of life which taught us survival. Numerous times we had to stand our ground, because older children never respected the younger ones. Meanwhile, my sister was getting older by the day and counted on me to be around more often. Our family was beginning to become stronger, and everyone from my father on down was on the same page.

I never forgotten my sister, or the day her breath was taken from life. My eye's watched the bullet pierce through her skin as it traveled through the wall, and seeing her body drop as blood splattered like paint to my face, blue jean jacket, and on the brim of my white t-shirt. Everything took place in slow motion not knowing her scream was from the pain she was dealing with from the bullet. My hands lifted up her arms while she laid there with no response, which gave me the sign that she no longer had control of her body. She was gone with every gut feeling I felt it was my fault, even though I didn't pull the trigger. Her blood began to range throughout the floors of the store, as I laid next to her screaming for her return. Her eye's remained open with no pain, worries, or voice while she took her last deep breath that signified I would see her in another lifetime. My strength laid her head down to the floor, and I kissed her one last time on the cheek and forehead knowing she was at peace. My tears stopped, because I couldn't cry anymore and my vision blurred because I couldn't see through the pain.

Cherishing every moment was my own sacred ground, and a protection within my heart. When I love an individual it seems like bad luck sat around the corner.

We were heading to the corner store that day, and rain poured heavily as we entered the old mildew smelling store filled with incense smoke, with dimmed lights from bad electric wires and light bulbs. I remember looking and laughing at my sister, while she grabbed her favorite peach soda and cheddar chips. We paid the cashier and began to walk towards the door when a man ran in. We never heard a gunshot, because the commotion was so loud and shocking. My body froze and I couldn't hear nor see. When I began to grab my sister I saw the bullet slide through her chest. The murderers were attempting to aim at someone else. My mouth couldn't speak, my ears couldn't hear, and my eye's couldn't see as my body shut down. She was five years old with a bright future and knowing she was a queen.

My father never was the same as he walked in silence months after. A sibling's loss was a hard pill to swallow and it takes a brave soul to handle it. Every day I expect my sister to run up behind me to follow every footstep that I took, or repeat every word that came out my mouth to drive me crazy. Missing things when it's gone, but not really appreciating it while it's here was a struggle I had to live with. . Her life on earth allowed me to see things clearly, because cherishing the moment is what we lack in as people. My sister love was unconditional as well as my mother's, and never could we get a life back nor could we get the time back that was missed.

Life provides us with only one first moment, as well as one second moment that could never be repeated or duplicated. My father's first child was different from his second child, because each experience was different. Moments or people we take for granted due to circumstances or ways we are set in. We forget the importance of family or friends, and diminish our moments of apologies and thank you's. My sister's last days were filled with love that we showed each other from our genuine heart's, not knowing that moment would of been our last hours, minutes, or seconds we would spend. While she roamed the earth I cherished the moments, because I wanted her to have a better life despite of how rocky mine was. Cherish every moment and know every day isn't guaranteed to anyone no matter the age, race, sex, or economic background.

EMPTY INSIDES
Chapter 8

My pain comes from the emptiness I have inside. Many let downs and hopeful moments inspired mixed feelings about my life. Different stages that I was forced to be in changed my emotional and mental state of mind. Most days I didn't know what to expect, because love from my father was good but not good enough. The loss of my sister played in my head everyday giving me this guilty conscious as if everything was my fault. My mother's absence had me feel the same as well, but a different kind of guilt because of her unwanted love she had for me. Changes in environments redeveloped my mind and helped me adapt to any habitat. Past experiences allowed me to be immune to anything that is thrown my way, and to be mentally tough.

I've had a lot of trials coming up in the inner city schools that made me want to relocate. Gang violence, bullying, drug infested neighborhood, prostitution, but most importantly child abandonment. I was lucky enough to have my father around to guide and teach my sister and me the value of respect. Unfortunately, my sister was slain due to gun violence, but I still felt I had to continue to guide her even though she wasn't physically here. My mother's presence was absent most of my life, and the love I needed from a woman was barely there even though I had a step-mother. My step-mother basically did the best she could, but my emptiness still weighed heavily on me and brought me down every moment I thought about it.

I'm in my adolescent years and the only thing I've been taught is how to be tough and responsible. The nurturing side never played a role, because a mother can only apply it. Forcing me to have puppy love was the only way I can succeed in filling the void. Boxes of chocolate, teddy bears, and cards at school dances were times that I took advantage of seeking what I needed. My behavior began to change, because my environment was influencing me. Hanging around the neighborhood kids taught me different ways of survival. Breaking in houses, stealing goods from hard working men, and learning how to lie to my father to get what I wanted were behaviors I picked up. My father glanced at me with no words spoken, and pretending as if he hadn't realized my reconstruction.

Every morning my father would take a forty-five minute jog around the neighborhood. Some days I would go, but laziness would take over my body so I would stay home and sleep. My father never abused me, but his talks were always intimidating enough.

After his jog, he entered my room and sat on the floor next to my bed.
"Son wake up let's talk, I noticed a lot of changes in your behavior and want to know what's going on with you", he said.

 "My mind is everywhere dad and I can't seem to find myself. Trying to find my mother and battling everything around me is very overwhelming", I replied.

We preceded our conversation, but I felt my life wasn't adding up. One day I will know the whole truth about my life, but when was a question that rang in my head.

The following morning the ray of the sun woke me out of my sleep. Football practice has been very intense, which causes me to sleep more due to my body developing. A long stretch and repeated tosses allowed me to finally get out the bed. I began to put my pajama pants on as I proceeded to walk down the stairs to get a glass of orange juice. As I approached the last step of the stairway, I heard my father on the phone. "This is your son too and your presence is needed if you know it or not" he said.

Patiently, I stood there for a moment before I continued my quest for orange juice. In my mind I was hurt, because he was debating with someone about me. My mother was the first thought I had in mind, and should I be mad at my father? My stomach turned from left to right, because I didn't know who he was talking too exactly or if I wanted to know. As I walked into the kitchen my father was astounded, because he thought I was asleep not realizing I heard the entire conversation.

My conscious entered my body and was anxious to know who my father was talking to. "Was it her", I asked as if I was scared of the response he would give. A long pause circulated through the room as if the world stopped, and I didn't feel ready to know the truth. My father didn't want to answer the question, but looked as if he was forced to talk to me. My mother's face surfaced through my mind as my father proceeded to speak. "Son there is a lot of things I need to tell you and I just want you to sit and listen", he said. I began to pour my orange juice and sat in the dining area anxious to know who I was. "Your mother's a drug addict that surfaces through this neighborhood every day, and countless times you have seen her. The reason we transitioned from a big house to this house was for you to be closer to her. My business that I own makes me a millionaire, but I wanted you to grow up in this type of environment for you to appreciate life and not take advantage of the world I want you to have. Basically, you are rich to, but I never want you to forget the importance of why I work or worked hard to get where I'm at. I wanted you to go through a lot of things as I've done, because if you never struggle you would never know how life really is. I love you and want the best for you, and that's the reason I've always been hard on you since you were born. I hope this gives you an insight of who we are as a family and help us move forward".

My mind was puzzled, but I felt better knowing the truth. My father waited late to tell me everything about my life, but it made me feel better to know through all these years why certain lessons were being taught. My mother has been back and forth out of rehabilitation, and at the times of battling her sickness was when she decided to call me. Those empty feelings became completed feelings, because now everything began to make sense. Knowing what my parents sacrifice will never be known, but the results show through their actions. I've learned to appreciate the lessons given and take heed to what you are taught while using it to make your life better than what theirs were.

WHEN NATURE CALLS
Chapter 9

Happiness never existed in my life consistently. The times my father embodied the worth of a man and thoughts of a worthless mother diminished the strength that held my head high. Nature calls in many ways, but the lessons you get will decide who you are and the outcome of how your life is revealed depending on how you react. During my little time on earth being exposed to different things were normal. Having a comfort zone wasn't a frame of a lifestyle, because I never knew what to expect. My cry was for every child that felt how I felt and every adult that never received the closure they deserved. Why do certain individuals go through the pain of neglect or any pain that isn't normal? We can't change our past circumstances, because maybe we are the tough ones that have to deal with the battles and struggles.

As I was being appreciative to life, it made me appreciate to nature. Beautiful animals, land, and the nature of a woman made the definition of life. As I found who I was, and knowing what I've gone through made me more comfortable with my life. Birds chirping, mist from the rain, heat from the sun, and the smell of fresh air symbolizes life. My father and I would take peaceful walks through the neighborhood with conversations about everything. I remember just falling asleep on the porch while seeing squirrels and birds chasing and fighting each other. Noticing different insects crawling completing a task, and knowing they have a certain purpose to make the world rotate. I watched animals on different channels killing prey or helping protect the ecosystem that may help this world one day.

Witnessing the birth of my deceased sister enabled a great deal of respect for what we call a woman. It was a blessing seeing how babies are conceived and the pain women go through to deliver them. One soul has the power to create a human being, but sometimes multiple at a time. The woman was made to handle the importance which is carrying a precious birth of life and be the strength of the world. In my neighborhood, I witnessed how men disrespected women, as well as women disrespecting themselves. My father always taught me the importance of respecting individuals due to the sacrifices people made just for us to breathe. Realizing how deep life is and where it takes you, allowed me to have a creative imagination. Daydreaming made me think of how powerful a mind could be in order for you to have the privilege to think. My mind wondered a lot especially seeing how vicious people were murdered just for protecting something that was theirs. It's funny how life goes, because as innocent as we are coming out of the womb of our mother; being murderers and thieves would never come into a mind of an innocent baby.

Road trips were always fun ever since I was younger. Throughout the trips we would stop at various gas stations for pit-stops. My favorite part about pit-stops was when I would buy my favorite drinks and snacks to prepare me for our long trip. Good music playing in the background, while having my own electronics or fun toys to play with were warm memories that I wish I still had. I watched my father look back at me through his rear-view mirror as he talked to my step-mother about various topics. As I've gotten older my father planned more trips, so that we could get out of the house. Going camping was something new to us, but the thought of sleeping outside gave me butterflies of not knowing what to expect. "Son I love nature, and I want us to get closer to it" was how my father presented the trip to me. Things my father would say or how it was said sometimes he was over excited. My thoughts were snakes, bugs, and bears but still I was willing to take on the challenge. We later headed to the wilderness store to buy fishing gear, tints, lighters, and other things that we thought was needed.

Meanwhile, we were packed up and ready to start our new adventure. Being city boys, we haven't had the experience of the country life. Survival skills are what my father had due to struggling most of his life, so he made nothing out of something. The preparation for this trip had nothing to do with my father's past experience, but I laughed in my head because my dad was always right. As we arrived at the site, trees and water was the only visual we had. Unfortunately, fear crossed my mind a little because we were in the middle of nowhere. My father was talking to me as if he knew what we were doing, but we bonded and laughed at little things that didn't matter. We learned how to fish, make fires, eat s'mores, and hiking. We both had no idea on what to expect but we always made ourselves have a good time. Spending time to live in the moment was what we needed, but being in the world of nature made it better.

Life reveals itself in many forms. The peacefulness that nature gives force us to love all creations for what they are. Sometimes I wonder why things happen whether good or bad.

Rain, storms, and other weather conditions are the same things that evolve around our lives as individuals. Our smiles equal the sun, the rain equals our tears, and storms equal the pain and suffering that we deal with throughout our lives. Our camping trip was much needed, because we had to get in touch with nature. Life balances to show that we all serve a different purpose, but same agenda. The child that gets murdered equals the child that's born, and from the father that teaches equals the father that walks away. My mother walked out the time she did to make my father stronger, and to teach me a different life. My sister was murdered in front of me to show me death doesn't have an age or time. If my mom would have stayed my father couldn't test how strong of a man he was, and if he could actually raise a boy into a man. It's funny how everything plays out, but when nature calls we have to sit back and answer the phone.

THE FAMILY
Chapter 10

My family was unstable with no consistency of love. I asked for too much that no human being could ever receive, which is a perfect family. My thought of a perfect family is dining diners with all silverware laid out with a feast of food, and everyone sitting around laughing and telling family stories. The fairy-tale way of life that brings the love out of every situation and grasp your thoughts of what you want your future to be. My family was nothing like I've dreamed or anyone else's dream.

Reality displayed a little bit more than what I have expected. Of course, my family wasn't the best, but we made the best of every situation. Having a fairy-tale life has its breakdown points more than an unstable family, because no family would ever be flawless. Every human wants a life that is perfect, but different characters in life are made for a reason to make us unequal. Personalities change the perspective of life, because every mind operates differently.

A ring from the doorbell caught my attention as I was getting ready to head to the park for a 1 on1 basketball session with a classmate. I finished packing the rest of my gym clothes and proceeded down stairs to see who it was. As I pulled the curtain back I noticed a woman standing on the porch anxious for the door to open. Hesitating to turn the knob I asked "May I help you". "Baby it's me" the woman replied with a smile that would change the world of someone maybe mine. My mind wondered to think if it was my mother. The moment I've been waiting for my whole life struck me at a time that I wasn't prepared for. Slowly the door open and tears ran down my face as she bent down to hug me. "I'm sorry" repeatedly came out of her mouth as she cried with me from anger, pain, and abandonment. Mentally, I didn't know how to think, feel, or act with my mind wondering into space.

Meanwhile, my family was slowly beginning to form and happiness embraced me with an overwhelming feeling. Forgiving my past was hard and I knew time will make it happen. Driving through the neighborhood my mom and I begin to talk about my accomplishments. I postponed my basketball session to spend the time I've always been waiting on. Time fly's when you're having fun and catching up on old times. Thinking of my absent mother my mind couldn't think back that far, because I was so excited for her to be in my presence. Our new beginning made me anxious for what our future holds.

My father and I begin this journey from the beginning with every memory being special and unforgettable. The teachings I've learned has brought me to the point of being humble. My mother is battling a sickness that is in most households, but it's up to me to keep her sane. We could never make someone remove themselves from drugs nor can rehabilitation make drugs exit a person's life. The individual have to know the importance of their life and that will result in their wellbeing for the future. My father agreed to allow our love to enter her life, so she can have something to look forward to. My stepmother respected my father's decision, because she loved my father and I enough to do anything to help

Trials bring a family together or it separates it deeply. My mother and father standing under the same roof at that moment like no problems were ever established. The memory of my sister plays in my mind, and explained why my stepmother walked in silence since that time. As strong as my father was that was the only moment I saw him breakdown in pain. My mother doped up trying to get the next hit not concerned about what's important. My mind troubled from emptiness, environmental changes, school, and mixed emotions about who I was. Through every change I've been through or saw we stuck together and stood strong despite of our personal weaknesses.

Questioning life is something that we shouldn't do, but we still find our way doing it. The things that we go through makes me think if everything was meant to happen, or do the people we involve in our lives influence it? Paths that we enter allow us to make a choice of different roads, but before we enter the roads the street sign always tell us where we are headed. Our destination is sometimes unlimited, because we tend to drive just to seek a direction. Do we turn around and choose a different street, the answer is no because we like taking risk.

Me and my father's journey has been a strange ride, but I love my father for what he stands for in my life and not giving up. Realizing how important he was didn't come until I sat back and thought about my experiences. My family is under one roof and one accord, which is looking forward. My stepmother has helped my mother tremendously in helping us direct her on the right path. How we were brought back together was strange, but the importance is that we are here finally. If someone ask me is my family perfect my answer would be no, but we understand each other and we are who we are. My life is a book that you may just see the cover, but the pages are burned, torn, damped, bloody, and stepped on.

To Be Continued...........

**ME AND MY FATHER'S JOURNEY
EDITION T-SHIRT**

AVAILABLE AT:
www.nwankwomishadtheauthor.com

Acknowledgements/Dedications

There is one name on the cover of this book, but there is a saying "It takes a village to raise a child". Many people have influenced me into how I think, act, and read. I would like to first thank my mother, Ms. Hughes which is the nucleus of my life. Her courage has raised men and women that have grown to be fearless despite of the outcome one my face. Her strength and the ability to be outspoken helped me develop the mindset that I have. I would like to give a special thanks to my siblings, which all of them played a huge role in pushing me as the middle child to be strong, courageous, and independent minded. I've learned how to think, be free under my own skin, and to have confidence.

My city of Benton Harbor, Michigan is the place that made me a soldier, and taught me to be more than what people expect of you. I would like to thank the real father's that lent their hand to help mold me into the man I've become including: my Cousins (Ed, Tommy, Johnny, Kenneth, Litt, Tony, Deon, and Wilbo), Uncles (Big Ed, Tracy, Don, Doniel, Sam, Nick, Slim, David, and Charles), and Coaches (Burton (BH), Porter (BH), and Randell (UAPB). I would like to send a special thanks to my brother Ahmad (Ajax Fitness and Nutrition), my cousin Tiesha Vassar (Make-up artist) and my girl Jas for listening to my ideas while helping me develop my thinking with constructive criticism. Those great individuals served a great purpose in my life that allowed me to write and express my personality and creativity. This book was inspired by lives I know and father's that actually taught their children whether coaching, mentoring, or parenting.

My second home Chicago, Illinois helped raise my mind and wisdom from what's true and false on how I view the world. I saw violence, gangbanging, drug users/sellers on another level that prepared me for my future. The University of Arkansas at Pine Bluff is where I received my Bachelors in Criminal Justice, but taught me more than just a degree. I developed my maturity and relationships with other people that will be forever indebted. The last city I would like to thank is Montgomery, Alabama which allowed me to take the wool off my eyes and know my purpose.

Last but not least, I would like to send a warm thanks to my son. He inspired, disciplined, taught me, and strengthened my relationship with God. Being a single father was the greatest test, because I didn't believe I could do it on my own but my faith guided us to work as a team. The powerful memories my son and I shared with all the trials we have faced will never be forgotten. His patience helped me continue to push myself.

Thank you readers for seeing my vision and creative thinking unfold. Everybody that showed their presence in my life negative or positive has been my inspiration to oversee my doubters and focus on my supporters. Thank you all with much love.

ABOUT THE AUTHOR

Nwankwo Mishad, a native of Benton Harbor, Michigan, was a resident of Pine Bluff, Arkansas. After graduating from The University of Arkansas at Pine Bluff, Nwankwo Mishad decided to enhance his writing ability, and turn them into stories. He has faced many obstacles that he has overcome that made him mentally and physically stronger. His respect for childhood challenges prepared him to become the man he is today. He has mentored children across the United States and continues to influence those that make their dreams exist. His street mentality helped him transfer his mindset into helping his communities and influence individuals to be positive no matter the circumstances we face as humans.

Me And My Father's Journey is Nwankwo Mishad's first book and he was determined to test himself to see if he could transition and become a versatile author. In high school, he wrote short stories for fun and never noticed his talents until his mother recognized his work. When he moved to Montgomery, Alabama he took a leap of faith where he became homeless while sleeping in his car and staying in and out of hotels. He never saw his purpose of relocating until his mind was clear to think in his darkest stages.

His inspiring words of wisdom given to neighborhood drug dealers, murderers, children needing guidance, and even his child inspired him to put his words to paper and send messages throughout his creative stories. He chose to write because his presence of a leader could influence his peers to pick up a book. His goals are to move this generation to continue to make their presence known, but use their rage into another element and take their influences to a level that will inspire others.

A PLACE CALL HOME

Benton Harbor, Michigan in my opinion is a creative and inspiring environment to be a product of. Despite of the current/past violence that can make you hate or want to distant yourself from it entirely. It is a place I call home and always stood proud to recognize it. We've faced many challenges that could make or break a person, but also help prepare for any experience that we may face throughout life.

Of course, other cites reflected my view of life, because every urban community is the same. The reality is that poverty that surrounded us made us react different in the way we live. It made us hungry and eager to explore different avenues that defined our individuality. We also became materialized to feel that if we wear a certain style of clothing/shoe people would respect us more. Sometimes the black community doesn't realize how much power we have when we think and invest in each other; instead we glorify a thing that kills us everyday which is material.

Mentally and physically society has formed us to hate, and feel we need things that can't bring us success. Unfortunately, most of us weren't granted with everything, and seeing people that we felt had everything formed us to be thieves and murderers to those that actually earned what they have legally or illegally. We had the neighborhood dope dealers that had the nice cars, plenty of women, or even all the money in the world exhibited a style that influenced everyone to be like them.

As children, we wanted what they had, but didn't see the problems they face. We also laughed at the addicts, as they behaviors changed while being high off the substances that were brought into our neighborhoods. Their entertainment was what the community made mockery of, but not knowing the sickness of death we were watching before our eyes On a positive note we have/had our neighborhood celebrity's .that inspired us to want change in the mindsets we held. People like: Benny Bowers, Maurice Burton, Marcus Muhammad, Lou Harvey, Robert Whaley, Wilson Chandler, Joique Bell, Pig, Courtney Burton, Ramsey Nickels, Shawn Shaw, Sinbad, Ernie Hudson, Michael Stokes, Zapp Sola, Honorable C-note, Young Monk, James Ferguson, Chi-Boy, and the list goes on. All these men in my community stood for something and taught us the necessary meaning of father's and role models. They also represented the growth of a man, especially coming from an environment that could mold us into destruction.

My twin brother (AJAX) and I saw the good and bad, and also knew how it felt to be loved and hated at the same time. I love my city with everything it has to offer. Michigan as a whole is one big family that supports each other from cities like: Grand Rapids, Flint, Detroit, Saginaw, Muskegon, Kalamazoo just to name a few. I represent for every struggle that is not afraid to make change. Shout to everyone that is in my generation that's carrying the torch to my city. We will continue to inspire.

-I AM BENTON HARBOR

THANK YOU!!

www.ingramcontent.com/pod-product-compliance
Lightning Source LLC
Chambersburg PA
CBHW070827250626
47170CB00006B/2233